REAL WORLD MATH

FIREFIGHTERS
to the rescue

Wendy Clemson and David Clemson

Tick Tock

An Hachette UK Company
www.hachette.co.uk
First published in the USA in 2013 by
TickTock, an imprint of Octopus Publishing Group Ltd
Endeavour House
189 Shaftesbury Avenue
London WC2H 8JY
www.octopusbooks.co.uk
www.octopusbooksusa.com

Copyright © Octopus Publishing Group Ltd 2013

Distributed in the US by
Hachette Book Group USA
237 Park Avenue
New York NY 10017, USA

Distributed in Canada by
Canadian Manda Group
165 Dufferin Street
Toronto, Ontario, Canada M6K 3H6

ISBN 978 1 84898 905 4

Printed and bound in China

10 9 8 7 6 5 4 3 2 1

Picture Credits
t=top, b=bottom, c=center, l=left, r=right, f=far
Peter Casolino/Alamy 10; Comstock Images/Alamy 30; FEMA/ Andrea Booher14-15; FEMA/ Justin Domeroski 16;
FEMA/ Bob McMillan 17; Shutterstock 1, 2, 3 (all), 4 (all), 5, 6-7, 8, 9, 12-13, 18-19, 20, 21, 22T, 22B, 23, 24,
26T, 26B, 27, 28, 29, 31T, 31B, 32; Jiang Jin/SuperStock 25
Cover: all Shutterstock except main image front cover by Flying Colours Ltd/ Getty

Every effort has been made to trace the copyright holders, and we apologize in advance for any unintentional omissions.
We would be pleased to insert the appropriate acknowledgement in any subsequent edition of this publication.

Contents

**MATH SKILLS COVERED
IN THIS BOOK:**

Numbers and the number system
Skip-counting by twos: p. 10
Fractions: pp. 12, 16, 25
Number line: pp. 16, 20
Number order: p. 13

Mental calculations
Addition and subtraction:
pp. 6, 8, 10–11, 16–18, 20, 23–24
Counting: pp. 12, 15, 28, 29
Division: pp. 6, 23
Multiplication: pp. 12, 17, 19, 23

Shape, space, and measurements
Comparing measures: p. 25
Compass N, S, E, and W: p. 14
Flat shapes (2-D): pp. 18, 28
Following directions: p. 11
Measuring with a ruler: p. 20
Position and direction: pp. 19–22
Scales and dials: p. 19
Telling time: p. 8

Organizing data
Bar graph: pp. 6, 28
Charts: pp. 8, 24
Interpreting data: pp. 25–26
Plans: p. 22
Picture graph: p. 15

Problem solving
Capacity: p. 17
Finding the difference: p. 9
Length: pp. 16, 20, 25
Time: pp. 8, 12, 17
Weight: pp. 19, 24
Figuring out costs: p. 24

**Supports math standards
for grades 2–4**

Welcome to the Fire Station

You are a firefighter at a busy fire station. You help to put out fires and rescue people in trouble. Your job is dangerous but it makes you feel good to help other people. Your skills and bravery save lives.

What does a firefighter do?

Most of the fires you put out are in homes, shops, and offices.

You also have to put out fires in the countryside.

You tell people how fires start and what they can do to stop them.

Sometimes you talk to children about your job.

But did you know that firefighters sometimes have to use math?

In this book you will find lots of number puzzles that firefighters have to solve every day. You will also get the chance to answer lots of number questions about fires, firefighters, and fire safety.

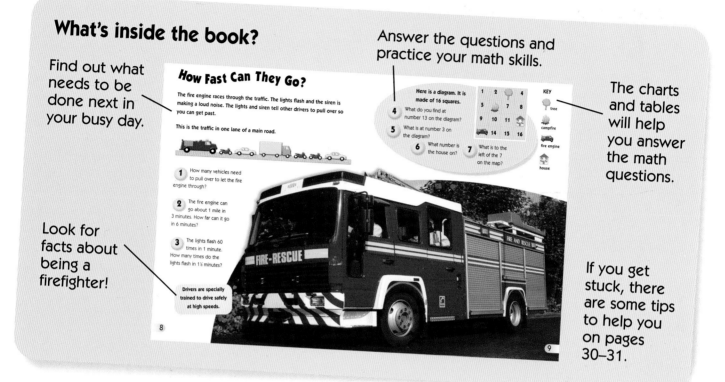

What's inside the book?

Find out what needs to be done next in your busy day.

Answer the questions and practice your math skills.

The charts and tables will help you answer the math questions.

Look for facts about being a firefighter!

If you get stuck, there are some tips to help you on pages 30–31.

How Fast Can They Go?

The fire engine races through the traffic. The lights flash and the siren is making a loud noise. The lights and siren tell other drivers to pull over so you can get past.

This is the traffic in one lane of a main road.

1. How many vehicles need to pull over to let the fire engine through?

2. The fire engine can go about 1 mile in 3 minutes. How far can it go in 6 minutes?

3. The lights flash 60 times in 1 minute. How many times do the lights flash in 1½ minutes?

Drivers are specially trained to drive safely at high speeds.

8

Here is a diagram. It is made of 16 squares.

1	2		4
5		7	8
9	10	11	
	14	15	16

KEY
- tree
- campfire
- fire engine
- house

4. What do you find at number 13 on the diagram?

5. What is at number 3 on the diagram?

6. What number is the house on?

7. What is to the left of the 7 on the map?

9

Are you ready to be a firefighter for the day?

You will need paper, a pencil, and a ruler, and don't forget to wear your firefighter's uniform! Let's go...

Your Fire Station

You are a firefighter in one of your town's fire stations. You could be called out to a fire at any time. You deal with all sorts of fires. Fires don't just happen in people's homes – there are plenty of fires in the countryside, too.

Here are the numbers of workers at a station.

2 fire chiefs – they decide how fires should be put out

2 crew leaders – they organize the firefighters

12 firefighters – they tackle the blaze

1 If these workers are in two equal teams, how many people are there in each team?

2 Your station is always busy! Last year you put out 130 big fires and 100 small fires. How many more big fires than small fires?

3 Your team put out 60 car fires and 15 house fires. What is the total number of car and house fires?

WHERE IS THE FIRE?

This graph shows the number of fires last month.

4 How many fires on farmland were there?

5 How many fires altogether?

Most fire stations have at least two fire engines.

Starting Your Shift

When you arrive at work, there are always lots of things to do, even when there are no fires. You have to make sure that everything on the fire engine works well. You keep the fire station clean and tidy.

Firefighters are needed night and day. They work in shifts. A "shift" is the time that a firefighter spends at work. It can be a day shift or a night shift.

1 This week you will work four day shifts. How many days in the week are you not working a day shift?

2 The clock shows the time in the morning that you start work. What time is it?

YESTERDAY'S TIMETABLE

You were not called out to a fire yesterday. Here is what you did instead.

9:00 to 10:30	Checked the engine
10:30 to 11:00	Break
11:00 to 12:00	Training
12:00 to 1:00	Cleaning
1:00 to 2:00	Lunch

3 What were you doing at 10:00?

4 What were you doing at 11:30?

5 What were you doing at 1:15?

6 After lunch, you spent another hour cleaning. Then you showed a group of children around the fire station until it was time to go home. You finished work at 5:00 p.m. How long did the visit from the children last?

NEW CLOTHES

Today you are getting a new uniform! The storeroom has lots of hats, pants, and jackets. You choose the clothes that fit you the best.

7 What is the difference between the numbers of helmets and jackets in the storeroom?

8 What is the difference between the numbers of pants and jackets?

14 helmets   36 pants   18 jackets

Uniforms protect firefighters from the heat. They are also waterproof!

The Alarm Call

Someone has dialled 911. There is a fire in town! The alarm bell at the fire station rings. All of the firefighters jump up and rush to the fire engine. It takes just 60 seconds for you to leave the station. You are on your way!

You aim to get from the fire station to the fire in 10 minutes.

1 Which of these puzzles have the answer 10?

A
1+2+3+4

B
2+2+2+2+2+2

C
180–160

D
30–3

E
2 x 5

2 A fire in the countryside takes 20 minutes to get to. How many groups of 2 in 20?

Specially trained operators take 911 calls. They find out details of the emergency and then let the fire station know.

3 The alarm bell sounds. It takes the firefighters one minute to get to the fire engine and leave the station. It then takes two minutes for them to reach the main road and three minutes for them to arrive at the fire. How long has it been since the alarm bell rang?

WHERE IS THE FIRE?

4 Look at the map of your town. You need to give the driver directions. Would you choose A, B, or C?

A Turn left out of the station, then left again, go past the traffic lights, and then right

B Turn right out of the station, then left, go past the traffic lights, and then turn left

C Turn left out of the station, then right, go past the traffic lights, and then turn right

How Fast Can They Go?

The fire engine races through the traffic. The lights flash and the siren is making a loud noise. The lights and siren tell other drivers to pull over so you can get past.

This is the traffic in one lane of a main road.

1 How many vehicles need to pull over to let the fire engine through?

2 The fire engine can go about 1 mile in 3 minutes. How far can it go in 6 minutes?

3 The lights flash 60 times in 1 minute. How many times do the lights flash in 1½ minutes?

Drivers are specially trained to drive safely at high speeds.

12

Here is a diagram. It is made of 16 squares.

1	2	🌳	4
5	🔥	7	8
9	10	11	🏠
🚒	14	15	16

KEY

🌳 tree

🔥 campfire

🚒 fire engine

🏠 house

4 What do you find at number 13 on the diagram?

5 What is at number 3 on the diagram?

6 What number is the house on?

7 What is to the left of the 7 on the map?

Forest Fire

There is a fire in the woods. In hot, dry weather, there is a big risk of fires. The dry wood and leaves mean there is lots of fuel for the fire. A strong wind can make a forest fire spread very quickly.

Firefighters check the direction of the wind. It is very dangerous to be in front of the fire if the wind is pushing it towards you.

Fire A

Fire B

1 Look at Fire A. The wind is blowing from north to south. Is the firefighter safe?

2 At Fire B, the wind is blowing from west to east. Is the firefighter safe?

A big wildfire can burn about 1 square mile in an hour.

14

A FIRE PICTURE GRAPH

Firefighters look for clues to figure out how the fire started. Here is a picture graph showing how forest fires started last year.

How the fire started	Number of fires
Lightning strike	🔥
Campfire	🔥 🔥 🔥 🔥 🔥
Deliberately started	🔥 🔥 🔥

🔥 = one fire

3 How were most fires started?

4 How many fires were there altogether?

5 Some trees die after a forest fire, but others can recover and have new leaves in the spring. How many of these trees are burned?

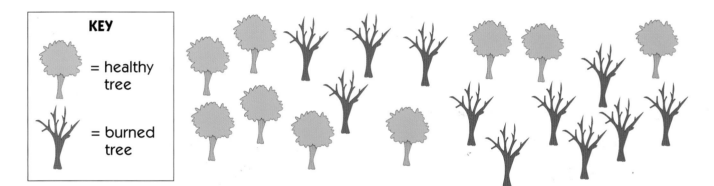

KEY

🌳 = healthy tree

🌲 = burned tree

15

On the Engine

The fire engine has all of the equipment you will need to tackle this forest fire. It carries long hoses and different sorts of ladders, as well as 500 gallons of water. The fire engine also has powerful lights to help the firefighters when they work in the dark.

The fire engine's ladders are 44½ feet long and 34½ feet long.

1 How much higher can the longer ladder reach?

You can see the first eight rungs of this ladder.

2 You are standing on rung 4 and move down 2 steps. What rung are you standing on now?

3 You are on rung 3 and climbs up 5 steps. What rung are you on now?

Firefighters make sure a fire is completely out in one area before moving on to the next.

The engine can pump about 10 gallons of water in 1 second.

4 How much water does it pump in 3 seconds?

Fire engines can carry about 3,000 feet of hose.

THE WATER TENDER

As well as engines, the fire station has a truck called a water tender. It can carry over 2,500 gallons! That is much more water than the engine can carry.

5 Fire engines have two hoses. Water tenders have five. How many hoses on two fire engines and one water tender?

The forest fire is out, but the station radios you. There is a fire in town – can you go straight there?

Rescue Mission

Time for your next call! You have arrived at the house fire. Before you can start to fight the fire, you need to see where the flames are coming from. Then you will check that everyone is safe.

This is the house that has a fire. You speak to the other firefighters to agree on how to tackle the blaze.

 1 Name these shapes:

A roof   **D** window to the left of the door
B door   **E** window to the right of the door
C top windows

Everybody is safely out of the building. But wait! You hear a barking sound – Rusty the dog is trapped upstairs. You quickly get out your ladder again. You're going to rescue him! You take:

2 minutes up the ladder   3 minutes in the house

1 minute to lift Rusty up   2 minutes to take Rusty to safety

2 How long does it take to rescue Rusty?

3 That dog is heavy! After the rescue, you put Rusty on some scales to see how much he weighs. How heavy is he?

4 Of course, people weigh much more than dogs. You once carried a woman from a burning building. She weighed as much as 3 Rustys! How heavy was she?

Your gloves have an inside layer that protects your hands from heat.

5 This is the back of one of your gloves. Is it for your right or left hand?

A fire grows quickly. It can double in size every minute.

19

Putting the Fire Out

There is no one in the building, and so you can now concentrate on putting out the flames. You use lots of water pumped through your hoses. You aim the hose at the bottom of the fire rather than at the flames. The fire is soon out.

In an emergency, firefighters take water from nearby ponds.

1 Your red hoses are 30 feet long. Your black hoses are 60 feet long. You can fit them together to make a longer hose. How many of each would you use to make a hose that was 90 feet long?

2 How would you make a hose that was 180 feet long? Use the fewest number of hoses.

3 Firefighters can choose the width of the hose as well as its length. This is the smallest hose. Use a ruler to measure it. How wide is the hose?

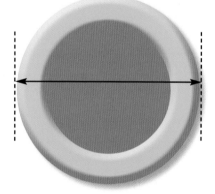

4 Bigger hoses are used to pump more water onto the fire. One is 3 inches across and another is 6 inches across. Look at this number line. Which letter marks the number 3?

5 What number does the letter D mark?

A   B   C   D

0   5   10

Firefighters can control the amount of water flowing through the hose as well as the pattern of the spray.

Cleanup Time

The fire is out, but is it safe to go back into the building? You and your team check that there is no chance of another fire starting. You also check that the building is safe for people to go into it.

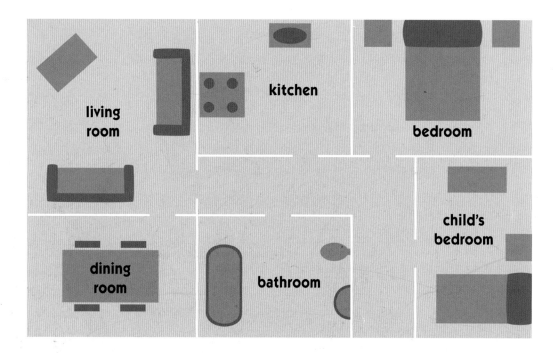

1. This is a plan of the house. You check that the fire is out in every room. How many rooms do you check?

2. You check the kitchen, living room, dining room, and then the bathroom. Are you going clockwise or counterclockwise?

3. How many rooms in this house are bedrooms?

After the fire there are lots of burned things to be thrown away. You help out and fill these things with garbage:

4 garbage cans   5 garbage bags   8 boxes

4 The numbers have been used in these puzzles. See if you can solve the puzzles.

A
5 + 8

B
8 – 4

C
4 x 5

D
8 ÷ 4

It's not just the fire that destroys homes – the heat, smoke, soot, and water cause damage, too.

After Work – Staying Fit

Firefighters need to be fit and strong. Each day on the job, they have to bend, stretch, lift, and carry. After work you exercise to make sure you can tackle any danger.

1 You have hand weights to lift. You would like a new set. You want a set that costs less than $17, and is not heavier than 10 pounds. Which set is best?

	Cost	Weight
Set 1	$10	11 pounds
Set 2	$20	10 pounds
Set 3	$15	8½ pounds
Set 4	$16	12½ pounds

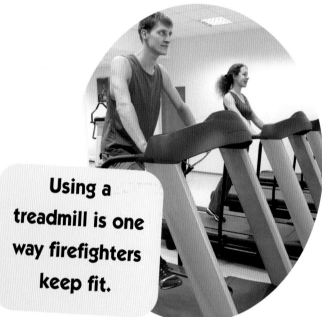

Using a treadmill is one way firefighters keep fit.

2 You use a jump rope to stay fit. You jump 35 times and then you jump 34 times. How many in all?

When you exercise, your heart pumps your blood around your body quicker. You can check your pulse to find out how fast your heart is pumping.

3 Before you start using the jump rope, your heart rate is 75 beats per minute. Afterwards, it's gone up to 92 beats per minute. How many beats has it gone up by?

4 You end your fitness time lying on your mat to relax. Are these sentences true or false?

A The mat is 2 feet wide

B The mat is 6 feet long

C The width is half of the length

48 inches

24 inches

Firefighters must be fit. The uniform and equipment weigh about 55 pounds – and that's before the firefighters have to rescue anybody!

In the News

Large fires are reported in the local newspaper. Your firefighting team is often mentioned. You talk to the reporters about what started the fire, how many people were rescued, and how you put the fire out.

YOUR LOCAL NEWS

Every Wednesday & Saturday

$1

People rescued from fire!

A brave firefighter rescued five people trapped in a burning building yesterday. The building on York Road caught on fire at seven o'clock last night. Nine firefighters tackled the blaze. They took one hour and eighteen minutes to put the fire out. The people trapped in the building were led to safety by firefighter Angie Jones. Angie, aged twenty-six, has been a firefighter for three years. Angie loves her job, and has put out forty-eight fires so far.

The fire started at 20 York Road. Two other buildings were also damaged by the fire.

1 How much does the newspaper cost?

2 How many times a week does the paper come out?

3 How old was Angie when she first became a firefighter?

4 What is the house number of the building where the fire started?

26

Look at the newspaper report. All of the numbers have been written as words. Write the answers to these questions in numbers.

5 How many firefighters tackled the blaze?

7 How long did it take the firefighters to put the fire out?

6 How old is Angie?

8 How many fires has Angie put out?

Firefighting is dangerous. Angie carries an alarm that will beep loudly if she becomes unconscious.

27

Staying Safe

Firefighters know what to do if they see a fire. Do you? If you see a fire, you should not try to put it out. Instead you need to raise the alarm. Shout "Fire! Fire!" very loudly, and get out of the building as quickly as you can. Then tell an adult, or dial 911.

HOW DID IT START?

This bar graph shows how some fires started.

1 How many fires were caused by a match or lighter?

2 What is the total number of campfire and barbecue fires?

3 What caused the fewest fires?

A   B   C   D

4 To stay safe we must read signs and understand what they mean. What shape are these signs?

A – danger!

B – read safety instructions below this sign

C – fire extinguisher

D – follow arrow to find fire exit

The gaps between the marks on the candles show one hour of burning time.

 5 If you burned the candles one after the other, for how long would you have light?

6 For how long would you have light if you burned both candles at the same time?

Enjoy fires safely. Remember, firefighters are happiest when there are no fires for them to put out!

Tips and Help

PAGES 6–7

Sharing and grouping – When we break up a number into equal groups, each group is a fraction of the whole number. Here each group is a team of firefighters.

Bar graph – A bar graph helps us compare information. In this case, the information concerns different kinds of fires. The graph shows how many of each kind of fire there were.

PAGES 8–9

Telling time – The little hand points to the hour. The big hand points to the minutes. When the little hand is between 8 and 9 and the big hand points straight down, the time is eight thirty (8:30).

Difference – Finding the difference is the same as subtracting. The difference between the numbers of helmets and jackets can be written as 18 – 14. Remember, in these subtractions we put the larger number first.

PAGES 10–11

Groups of two – When working with groups of two, it helps to learn the pattern of counting by twos like this:
Zero 2 4 6 8 10 12 14 16 18 20 22 24

Following a map – It can help to follow a map if you turn the map to match the direction you are going. Turn the book around if you need to, so that the road is facing the way you want to go.

PAGES 12–13

Half – The symbol for half is ½. The bottom number tells the number of equal parts in the whole. The top number tells the number of parts you have.

PAGES 14–15

Compass points – N, S, E, and W (north, south, east, and west) are called the points of the compass. A compass shows which direction is north. It can help us find our way and talk about direction.

Picture graph – A graph in which a picture is used to show one or more than one thing. In this picture graph a flame picture means one fire.

PAGES 16–17

Number line – The ladder here is like a number line. It is as though there is a number on each rung. You can use the number line to count forward and backward (or up and down the ladder).

PAGES 18–19

Naming shapes – To help name flat shapes, look at their sides and corners:

Square four sides all the same length and four right-angle corners

Rectangle two pairs of sides the same in length and four right-angle corners

Triangle three sides

Circle every point on a circle is the same distance from its center: a circle has no angles

Scales and dials – In math these help us measure. We need to look very carefully to check that the unit is correct. For example, these scales show us pounds.

PAGES 24–25

Reading a table – When we collect information and write it in lists, we call this a table. Here the lists are side by side, so that we can compare them. In this table you can compare the four sets of hand weights.

Foot – There are 12 inches in 1 foot.

PAGES 20–21

Measuring with a ruler – To measure the width, be sure the zero, or left, edge of the ruler lines up with the end of the left-pointing arrow. The number where the right-pointing arrow ends is the width of the hose.

PAGES 26–27

Words for numbers – Remember numbers can be written in words like "one, two, three…" and figures or symbols. We use just ten symbols to write all numbers. The symbols are 0 1 2 3 4 5 6 7 8 9. Where we put each symbol shows its value. So the one in the number 123 is one hundred, in 12 it is one ten, and in 31 it is one one.

PAGES 22–23

Clockwise – Clockwise is the direction in which the hands of a clock move around.

Counterclockwise – Counterclockwise is the other way around.

PAGES 28–29

Signs – It is important to be able to read signs. Spot them in buildings, in the street, and in your home. They are often warnings. Pay attention to the picture in a sign. Signs may have the same shape but different pictures.

Answers

PAGES 6–7

1	8 people	**4**	4 fires
2	30 fires	**5**	15 fires
3	75 fires		

PAGES 8–9

1	3 days	**5**	lunch
2	8:30 a.m.	**6**	2 hours
3	checking the engine	**7**	4
4	training	**8**	18

PAGES 10–11

1	A and E	**3**	6 minutes
2	10	**4**	C

PAGES 12–13

1	6 vehicles	**5**	tree
2	2 miles	**6**	12
3	90 times	**7**	campfire
4	fire engine		

PAGES 14-15

1	no	**4**	9 fires
2	yes	**5**	11 trees
3	campfire		

PAGES 16–17

1	10 feet	**4**	30 gallons
2	Rung 2	**5**	9 hoses
3	Rung 8		

PAGES 18–19

1	A triangle	**2**	8 minutes
	B rectangle	**3**	40 pounds
	C rectangles	**4**	120 pounds
	D square	**5**	right hand
	E circle		

PAGES 20–21

1	1 black hose and 1 red hose, or 3 red hoses	**3**	2 inches
		4	B
2	3 black hoses	**5**	6

PAGES 22–23

1	6 rooms	**4**	A = 13
2	counterclockwise		B = 4
3	2		C = 20
			D = 2

PAGES 24–25

1	Set 3	**4**	A true
2	69 jumps		B false
3	17 beats per minute		C true

PAGES 26–27

1	$1	**6**	26
2	twice a week	**7**	1 hour and 18 minutes
3	23		
4	20	**8**	48
5	9 firefighters		

PAGES 28–29

1	6 fires		C square
2	5 fires		D rectangle
3	campfire	**5**	11 hours
4	A triangle	**6**	6 hours
	B circle		